# The Hermit of Fog Hollow Station

"If Old Man Turner catches you, he'll fry your heart for supper."

That's how the two local boys warned newcomer Alex as they led him off on a fishing expedition. And sure enough, they'd hardly hooked their first sunfish before the hulking old man appeared from behind the swamp and began to chase them.

But the chase ended as abruptly as it began when the old man collapsed with a heart attack, and Alex found himself, instead of fleeing, turning back to help.

That was the beginning of a strange relationship between the lonely boy and the crabby, self-sufficient old recluse. Alex visited Mr. Turner in the hospital, then in the deserted railroad station he called home. At first the old man was hostile and contemptuous, but little by little he warmed to Alex, and in time the two became friends.

For Alex, a new world opened—to ideas and ways of thinking that had never occurred to him before. For Mr. Turner, a rare thing came into his life at its very end—a friend and an heir. Each gave to the other, each gained, until the final loss.

Here is the gentle story of an unusual friendship that brought two hearts together across the barrier of the generations. Its universal appeal should attract readers of every age and state of mind.

# DAVID ROTH

# The Hermit of Fog Hollow Station

BEAUFORT BOOKS, INC.
*New York*     *Toronto*

No character in this book is intended to
represent any actual person; all the incidents of the
story are entirely fictional in nature.

Library of Congress Cataloging in Publication Data

Roth, David.
The hermit of Fog Hollow Station.

SUMMARY: Lonely after his family moves from Boston
to the country, 12-year-old Alex befriends an old hermit.
[1. Moving, Household—Fiction. 2. Hermits—Fiction.
3. Friendship—Fiction] I. Title.
PZ7R7275He  1980      [Fic]      80-22241
ISBN 0-8253-0012-6

Published in the United States by Beaufort Books, Inc.,
New York. Published simultaneously in Canada by
Nelson, Foster and Scott Ltd.
Designer: Ellen Lo Giudice

Printed in the U.S.A.      First Edition
10  9  8  7  6  5  4  3  2  1

2126547

For Cilla, who helped me find
the writing after I had lost it.

# one

They came the second week Alex was living in the new house and introduced themselves by charging him from behind and tackling him to the ground. They ran so quickly out of the bushes between his yard and the railroad tracks behind his house that Alex barely had time to look around before his face was down in the tall grass.

"You were too easy," one of them said. "Come on, Benny, let him up."

Alex scrambled to his feet and looked at both of them warily. The thin one with deep brown eyes stuck out his hand.

"I'm Fritz Holmer. This is Benny." Fritz nodded toward the fat boy beside him. Benny didn't offer his hand, but stood there regarding Alex from a sideways angle, not meeting his eyes.

"We're your neighbors," Fritz told him. "The gray house down by Four Corners." He turned to stare critically at the old farmhouse on a rise above the backyard. "Whatever made your folks buy this place?"

Alex felt his face flush. "We're going to restore it."

"With a stick of dynamite?" Fritz laughed and looked at Benny, who took his cue and laughed with him.

Alex clenched his fists. He hated the house his parents had bought, hated the move from Boston to this empty dirt road in the middle of abandoned fields and overgrown woods—but he would never let these two know he felt this way. Their laughter made him want to defend his parents' choice as if it were his own.

"What's your name?" Fritz asked.

"Alex Webb."

"How old are you?"

"Twelve."

Fritz nodded. "We're both thirteen. You'll probably go to junior high at the Central School in September. That's where I'm going. Benny here is a dummy and stayed back twice."

Benny squirmed under the look Fritz gave him. "Go to hell. I ain't dumb."

Benny was larger than Fritz, not just heavier, but taller and broader across the shoulders. Despite this, Fritz was the obvious leader. Alex studied them, trying to decide if he wanted to know them any better, wondering how he would get rid of them if he didn't.

"You are a dummy," Fritz was telling Benny. "Anybody could have passed sixth grade with Mrs. Olson, anybody except you."

"How come you talk to your brother like that?" Alex asked.

8

Fritz snarled his answer. "He ain't my brother! He just lives with us. He's a *foster* child," he sneered.

Around them the summer afternoon buzzed with insects. Alex swatted a mosquito on his arm. The sun poured down its heat upon them, and the grass around them smelled warm and green. Alex felt the hate smoldering in Benny when Fritz teased him. He decided he didn't like either of them very much.

"What's this for?" Fritz asked Alex, looking at the stake Alex had been pounding into the ground.

"Horseshoes."

"Need a sand pit for that. Ain't no good trying to throw horseshoes in this grass."

"It's good enough for me." Alex picked up the sledgehammer and angrily pounded the top of the metal stake. The hammer glanced off and just missed his foot.

Fritz laughed. "Come on, forget that. Got a fishing pole?"

Alex nodded.

"Go get it. We'll show you a good place to fish. We left our poles down by the tracks."

Alex hesitated. He didn't like them, but he didn't know how to say no without seeming stuck-up. And they were the only kids he'd seen in the two weeks he'd lived in North Letford. They might be the only friends he'd make all summer.

This thought brought a stabbing memory of his best friend Charlie back in Boston. He would probably never see Charlie again, and Charlie hadn't written yet, even though Alex had written to him twice.

"Come on," Fritz said. "You can play horseshoes any time."

Alex looked at Benny, to see if anything else lurked under

the slowness and the scowl. Suddenly Benny grinned at him.

"We got the worms," he said. "We'll share them with you."

"Okay," Alex said. "Wait till I get my pole."

"We'll meet you by the tracks," Fritz told him.

Alex nodded and ran up the small hill to his house. He was surprised how excited he felt at the thought of not spending another afternoon alone. Charlie and Boston were gone. Maybe there would be more to like about Fritz and Benny once he got over their strange ways.

His fishing pole was leaning up in his closet behind a pile of boxes. There were boxes in every closet in the house and in the corners of every room.

While he was pulling the boxes in his closet aside to get the pole, his mother came upstairs and looked in his room. She had reddish-brown hair like his, cut nearly as short as his, and they shared the same hazel-colored eyes, the same shaped nose, mouth, and chin. Alex often wished he didn't look so much like his mother, for everyone said how pretty she was. Alex sometimes stood before a mirror when he was sure he was alone and tried to contort, push, and twist his face into the comfortable homeliness his father enjoyed.

His mother had white paint on her nose and a brush in her hand. "Are you going off with those boys?"

"Yeah." He leaned the fishing pole against the wall and began repiling the boxes.

"Go ahead, honey" his mother said. "I'll get those. You don't want to keep your new friends waiting."

"They're not my friends, yet."

His mother looked at him and shrugged. "Well, don't keep them waiting, Alex."

Alex picked up his pole, ducked her kiss, and pounded down the stairs.

"Don't be late for supper," his mother's voice came floating down behind him.

He grunted a reply she'd never hear. Outside he looked for Fritz and Benny but couldn't see them down by the tracks. Probably they were gone already; that might not be a bad thing, considering how strange they were.

But then he felt lonely again and hurried across the yard. During the days before the move, during all the endless talk of the new house, the new life-style they would have once they left Boston, Alex had hidden a private loneliness stronger than any emotion he had ever felt before. When his sister decided to stay behind, keep her job, and go back to college in the fall, he had desperately hoped she would ask him to live with her. But she hadn't, and the time to leave had come, and it had all been worse than he had imagined. . . .

He found the path through the bushes that led onto the gravel beside the tracks. Far ahead he could see Fritz and Benny walking the rails. Fritz turned and waved to him.

"Come on, Alex!" he shouted.

Alex hurried to catch up, skipping over the ties between the rails. The air smelled of hot tar, and the rusty rails still gleamed on top from the passage of the freight train that came through each night.

Far ahead, Fritz and Benny, each balanced precariously on a rail, raced to keep ahead of him.

# two

"Place we're going," Fritz told Alex when he finally caught up with them, "it's off limits, so we got to be careful."

"What do you mean?"

Benny laughed. "Old man Turner catches you there, he'll fry your heart for supper."

"Who's old man Turner?" Alex looked uneasily around him, but the scrub brush ran uninterrupted along each side of the tracks. Only the red-winged blackbirds watched them go by.

"He's a hermit," Fritz said. "Lives in an old railroad station down the line from here. But we're going to cut off into the woods and get to his pond from the side so he don't see us."

"Fog Hollow Station," Benny said, something round and awful creeping into his voice. "Old man Turner, he's lived there for years and years, since when the passenger trains stopped running. Only freights go by now, and they never stop. So he's got the station all to himself."

Alex shifted his fishing pole into his other hand. He watched the rails ahead disappearing into a long curve. "What's he look like?"

"He's big and mean, with a dirty yellow beard and long fingers and—"

Fritz punched him in the shoulder. "You never been close enough to see his fingers! Only times you been near him, you been running so fast the other way, you don't know what he looks like."

Benny scowled at him but said nothing.

Fritz pointed with his fishing pole as they followed the tracks out of the curve. "Beyond the trestle, you can just see the corner of the station behind those dead elm trees."

Alex looked but saw nothing other than the trees. "Why do they call it Fog Hollow Station?"

Fritz stared at him a moment, then shook his head. "Because that's its name! Are you another dummy like Benny here? Got an old signboard nailed up on the front of the station, says Fog Hollow Station. It's always been called that, account of the way the fog gathers on the pond and the swamps behind the station."

They crossed the trestle. Alex stepped carefully from tie to tie, trying not to look down at the stream that flowed fifteen feet beneath the tracks. On the other side they paused a moment, looking in the direction of the station. Alex could see the weathered gray wood shingles and a section of roof beyond the elm trees.

"Don't worry," Fritz told him as he led the way down

the embankment to a narrow path that entered the woods. "Old man Turner is just a mean old man that don't want nobody near his place. Thinks he owns the whole woods. He's chased us plenty of times. But he's never caught us yet."

They were on the same side of the tracks as the station, but once in the woods, Alex lost all sight of it. The trees swallowed them up, oaks and beech trees forming a high archway above the narrow, single-file path. Occasionally the path would join the stream they had crossed at the trestle and would run along its bank for a little way before burying itself in the forest again.

Alex had worked up a sweat on the tracks, and he shivered now in the cool damp of the woods. They had lost the afternoon somewhere above them in the trees and were walking in a green, dark twilight. They did not find the afternoon again until they emerged from the path beside a large, blue pond.

"Loaded with fish," Fritz told him. "Trout, bass, pickerel. You name it, we've got it in that pond."

They climbed onto a dead tree trunk that lay like a dock in the water. Benny brought out a small can of worms from his shirt pocket and they took turns baiting their hooks.

Looking around, Alex could see nothing of Fog Hollow Station from here, just the woods that crowded the pond on three sides and a swamp on its south side stretching off into a tangle of dead trees.

"Beaver," Fritz said, nodding toward the swamp. "They back up the water pretty good." He cast his line and began reeling it slowly in.

As they fished, Fritz and Benny told him the legends surrounding the hermit of Fog Hollow Station. Their stories gave him cold shivers despite the heat of the afternoon that hovered over the pond.

"Two kids have disappeared in the time he's been living there," Fritz told him. He paused long enough to reel in a small sunfish, take it off the hook, and throw it back. "They were last seen near these tracks and never no sign of them after that."

Benny laughed a high-pitched, nervous laugh. "People say old man Turner caught them snooping around his place and cut off their heads and smoked them in his smokehouse just like hams and ate them all winter."

Alex tried to shrug off the story. "Maybe they just drowned in the pond here. Or got lost in the woods."

"Then how come their bodies were never found?" Benny demanded. He looked at Alex as if to dare him not to believe him.

Fritz cast his line again expertly, far out toward the middle of the pond. "Fact is, whether he ate them or not, they disappeared nearby and he claimed never to have even seen them around. Lots of people in town, they think the old man ought to be burned out."

"Why should he kill kids just for sneaking around his place?"

"To protect his hoard, that's why."

Benny nodded his agreement. Alex couldn't be sure if Fritz really believed the stories he was telling or was having fun at Alex's expense, but Benny obviously believed every word of them.

"People say he's got a chest full of old silver coins hidden away in the station," Fritz said. "Been saving them for years and years. Lives like a poor man but he's rich.'' This last he said with disgust in his voice, as if to live poor by choice was the most insane act of all.

It was getting late, and all they had caught so far was a few sunfish. The two Alex had caught had thrilled him even so, but he had been reluctant to show this, for Fritz and Benny were so scornful of these small, golden fish. He was ready to leave, but Fritz wanted to try their luck a little longer.

"Gets better later in the afternoon,' he said. "Long shadows bring out the big ones.''

Alex caught another sunfish. It gleamed wet and bright in the sunlight when he reeled it in. As he was carefully releasing it, he felt Benny stiffen beside him.

"It's him!'' he hissed. "Old man Turner! Over near the swamp!''

Alex looked up and saw a large, hulking figure watching them from some high ground in the swamp. Without a sound he began walking with long strides toward them, stepping down through the wet ground seemingly without noticing the water, his face hidden by the tangle of his white beard.

"Let's go!'' Benny shouted, starting them all scrambling off the tree trunk they had been fishing from. Alex dropped his pole, and by the time he had retrieved it, the other two were at the edge of the trees. Glancing back, he saw the old man gaining rapidly.

"Wait for me!'' he shouted, but he knew even through his fear that they wouldn't wait. He raced up the path, blundering into branches in his haste, his heart pounding.

He caught up with them beside the stream. They had started crossing to the other side, and Fritz had slipped on the rocks.

"Goddamn old man!" he was bellowing over and over again. His forehead was bleeding as he splashed the rest of the way across the stream and up the far bank.

Alex thought he could hear the old man breathing hard behind him. He waded through the water and joined Fritz and Benny on the other side.

"Where is he?" Benny asked in a loud whisper.

Alex tried to shush him, but Fritz was still swearing loudly anyway. He had a handful of rocks.

"If he comes around that bend, I'm going to let him have it!" Fritz shifted all the rocks to his left hand except one. "I mean it!"

Everything happened so quickly then that Alex felt lost in a whirl of events beyond his control. Old man Turner strode from the shadows of the trees, saw them across the stream, yelled something unintelligible, and charged into the water. Benny squealed in fear and bolted—but Fritz held his ground and threw his first rock.

His second rock struck the old man in the shoulder. He was so close now that when he looked up at them, Alex saw him clearly for the first time. The old man's eyes looked into his as no one had looked at him before.

Alex reached out to stop Fritz. "Don't throw any more rocks," he said, still transfixed by those eyes. They seemed to bore into him and read his soul. They seemed to say something he couldn't understand.

And then a look of anguish swept across the old man's face. He doubled forward and fell into the stream.

# three

---

"Don't go near him," Fritz yelled as he hurried after Benny. "It's a trick."

Then Fritz was gone, followed by the sound of his own steps running through the woods, breaking twigs, at last fading away.

Alex looked down at the stream. Old man Turner had fallen on his side, his face half in the water. Alex hesitated for just a moment, thinking that this might be a trap, that the old man might spring on him the moment he came close. But he would drown if Alex didn't pull him from the water, and his eyes still burned in Alex's mind.

Lying in the stream, the old man looked like a huge, wounded beast. His denim overalls and plaid shirt were stained dark with water and his left hand had sprawled out on the rocks, its long, thick fingers curled into a claw. Expecting any moment to be trapped by the old man's arms, Alex reached down and carefully pulled him over. The old man's face was a pasty gray above the beard and his eyes seemed not to see through the slits under his eyelids. Alex took a deep breath to calm his frightened heart and pulled the old man out of the stream.

It was all he could do to get the upper part of his body out of the water. He had to leave him there propped against the bank, from where he would hopefully not fall forward again and drown. Alex looked again to be sure he was breathing, for the rapid, shallow breaths moved his chest so slightly.

Alex glanced around as if the trees might tell him what to do next. But he knew that he couldn't leave the old man here to die. He had to go for help. He pulled the man securely against the stream bank one last time, then turned without another look back and trotted along the path to the tracks.

Fritz and Benny were nowhere to be seen. Alex hesitated for a moment once he had climbed the embankment to the tracks. He couldn't go home—their telephone hadn't been installed yet. Maybe the old man had a phone at the station.

As he ran along the tracks, he wished with all his might that he had never gone fishing with Fritz and Benny. His lonely game of horseshoes looked ever so inviting now. But now was too late. He was the only one who could get help for the old hermit, whether he was a man or a monster.

The railway station lay silent and weather-beaten in the long rays of the afternoon sun. As Fritz had described to him, there was a signboard high on the front of the building facing the tracks. On it was lettered in faded paint: FOG HOLLOW

STATION. There was an air of neglect and abandonment that hovered over the building and over the gravel and cinder yard around it. The weeds raised spiky heads into the afternoon breeze as if no one cared how high they grew. It seemed impossible to Alex that anyone lived here—anyone human, that is.

But the front door, which he reached by vaulting up onto a narrow deck not served by stairs, opened to his touch. Inside the air smelled stale and smoky, as if a fire smoldered there all year. In the light from two partially boarded-up windows Alex gave the front room a quick search, then went into a kind of kitchen. There was an old wood range against the far wall and a table missing a leg propped against a windowsill to keep it from toppling over with its burden of books, magazines, and dirty dishes. A pail of water stood on another table near a door that was ajar on the back steps. A board rattled somewhere in the wind.

There was no refrigerator, no electric lights, no telephone. Fascinated by the evidence of such a dark, disordered life, Alex had to physically shake himself in order to pull away. He retraced his steps through the dark front room and jumped down onto the ground again.

Looking across the tracks, he saw a narrow dirt road that left a flat area of caked mud near the tracks and climbed the hillside beyond. He ran to it and on, until he became winded, then walked the rest of the way. It came out on his own road, about a mile and a half south of his house. One of the few other houses that shared his road occupied the edge of a field across the way.

He hurried over and pounded on the front door. An elderly, white-haired woman finally answered and looked at him in amazement through the screen door as he told her about the hermit. When he realized she was hard of hearing, he repeated his story more slowly.

"But who are you, boy?" she kept interrupting him to ask.

When he had explained to her satisfaction just who he was and where he lived, she nodded.

"I'll call Chief Bicks," she said and disappeared into her house, leaving Alex standing on her granite stoop.

He could hear her shouting into the phone from somewhere inside the house, and he wondered if the town policeman was deaf, too. Then she reemerged and pointed to a rope swing hanging from a high oak tree.

"Chief Bicks told me to have you wait right here until he gets here," she said primly. She stood in her doorway while he walked over to the swing and sat down on it to wait. Her eyes, far sharper than her hearing, watched him closely until she was satisfied that he wasn't going to run off.

Her attitude toward him made Alex feel all the more guilty. As he waited for the policeman, he remembered the events of the afternoon and tried to assess his own blame in the affair. He realized that even if he had refused to go fishing with Fritz and Benny, they would have gone without him, and the afternoon would have spun itself out in the same way. Except that old man Turner might have drowned, Alex thought, because Fritz and Benny would have left him there.

But still he felt to blame, as if just by being there, he had caused all this to happen, had made a feud begun long before his move to North Letford come to such a terrible result.

The old woman appeared at her door again to see that he was still waiting there. He waved, wishing desperately that she would smile, but she didn't.

He saw his father drive by on his way home from work. He jumped off the swing and waved and shouted, but there was no reason for his father to look this way, and soon the car had disappeared in a cloud of dust.

He would be late for super. Trouble was closing in on him like a cold fog. He sank down dejectedly onto the swing and tried to ignore the old woman staring at him from her doorway.

# four

Chief Bicks arrived a few minutes after his father drove by, in a battered green pickup with a blue light clamped to a roof rack above the cab. The chief himself was short and powerfully built with bristly gray hair and a whiskery face. He jumped from the truck with a quick glance in Alex's direction, then hurried up the path to talk to the old woman. In his stained, patched work clothes, he shared something of the dilapidated look of his truck.

After a few words on the granite stoop, Chief Bicks again looked at Alex, then politely tipped his cap toward the woman behind the screen door and hurried over to the swing.

"I'm Chief Bicks," he said, sticking out a large, powerful hand. "You must be the Webb boy. Your folks just bought the old McDaniel place?"

Alex nodded, too surprised at first by the smile and the offered hand to extend his in return.

"Come on, boy, give me the mitt," Chief Bicks said at last. "I don't bite. What's your first name?"

"Alex."

"Okay, Alex. While we wait for the boys from Meadow Lawn to get here with the ambulance, suppose you fill me in on what happened."

Alex told him as simply as he could, carefully leaving out Fritz's and Benny's names and any mention of the rock throwing.

Chief Bicks grunted when he had finished. His chilly gray eyes didn't smile when his face did, despite the wrinkles around them. "Fishing in the pond, eh?"

Alex nodded.

"Fritz Holmer and that kid Benny Reeves who lives with him, they the ones with you?"

When Alex hesitated, Chief Bicks patted him on the shoulder.

"You're not tattling, Alex," he said. "I'd guess they were both there even if I didn't have you here to tell me so. Any trouble within ten square miles of here and them two are mixed up in it some way. Especially involving old man Turner. After this, you'd best stay clear of them."

Chief Bicks heard the ambulance coming up the road and hurried out to flag it down. Then he waved Alex over to his pickup.

"You ride with me. We'll follow them down to the tracks. Then you can lead us to the old man."

Bouncing from rut to rut, they followed the ambulance

down the narrow dirt road to the caked patch of mud by the tracks opposite Fog Hollow Station. There the ambulance laboriously turned around, and then Alex led Chief Bicks and the two attendants with the stretcher along the tracks and down the path into the woods.

Old man Turner had pulled himself out of the stream while Alex was gone after help, but he had made it no farther than a grove of small oaks. Sitting against one, he looked at them with frightened eyes as they came up. His face was tight and colorless, his forehead beaded with sweat.

"Mr. Turner, you just rest easy," Chief Bicks said gently. "These boys here will take you over to the hospital at Milton Falls and we'll have the doctors there give you a checking over."

Old man Turner tried to get up, but the strength wasn't there in his legs, and he fell back against the tree. The frightened look never left his eyes, and Alex wondered if he understood what Chief Bicks had told him.

The ambulance attendants quickly lifted him onto their stretcher as if he were no more than a bundle of old clothes. In a few moments they had disappeared up the path with their burden.

Chief Bicks looked carefully around at the woods as if he expected to spy a new witness to the crime between the oak trees and the birches, then put his arm around Alex's shoulders.

"We'll just let them ambulance boys do their business and we'll do ours. That your fishing pole over there?"

Alex nodded. He had completely forgotten about it.

"Better get it," Chief Bicks said. "Before it disappears."

He led the way slowly back to the railroad tracks. Alex was

eager to be away and home but felt somehow that he could not go until Chief Bicks dismissed him. When they reached Fog Hollow Station, Chief Bicks took off his cap and scratched his head.

"What I got to do, Alex, is take a quick look in there to make sure he didn't leave nothing burning or such, then we'll put on a couple padlocks to keep out our friends Fritz and Benny." He looked at Alex and winked. "Good friends as we both know they are. Want to help me?"

Alex nodded.

"You're one quiet boy, you are," Chief Bicks said, looking at the sky. A hawk circled far overhead, riding a fading thermal. Afternoon was ending, and the evening shadows were gathering near Fog Hollow Station, ready to engulf it.

Together they looked through the station. There was no fire in the wood stove, no lamps had been left lit. Finally, outside, Chief Bicks got two padlocks from his truck, and they placed one on the front door, one on the back.

Evening was coming fast. Alex looked down the tracks toward home.

"I got to get home," he said at last.

Chief Bicks nodded. "I'll give you a ride. I imagine an explanation from me might keep your folks from bearing down on you too hard."

They returned to the truck and Alex put his fishing pole in back. Chief Bicks drove slowly up the narrow lane to the road above. Looking out, Alex felt sudden hot tears burn into his eyes, and he had to force them back.

"What's going to happen to old man Turner?" he asked.

Chief Bicks turned to look at him a moment. His gray eyes for the first time relaxed with his smile.

"I don't know, Alex, me boy. Probably his heart give out while he was chasing you and Fritz and Benny. He's no youngster. Only the doctors can tell us how bad it is."

"I didn't know . . . " Alex couldn't finish.

"All this was going on long before you moved here."

They were on the main road, heading north toward his house. Alex studied the trees beyond his window, biting down hard on his lower lip to stop its trembling.

"Mr. Turner, he's what we call around here a real peculiar character," Chief Bicks said. "And people like him, who are different, well, Alex, they don't make out so good, even away out here in the boondocks. They attract troublemakers the way a lightning rod attracts lightning."

"You mean he's not . . . " Alex searched for a word that wasn't cruel. "He's not all there?"

"He's sharper than you and me put together," Chief Bicks said emphatically. "I've had many a conversation with him when I've come across him out on the roads on one of his walks. The head is there, but something's wrong in the heart. I don't mean physically, like what happened today. I mean, he's never talked about it and there's more stories floating around here than coons in a cornfield in August, but something broke that man's heart years ago and he's never got over it. He's hid himself away in that old station by the tracks, but whatever demon plagues him, it's living right there with him every day."

Chief Bicks drove into the driveway beside Alex's house. Alex turned to him and quickly asked his question.

"Fritz and Benny, they said old man Turner killed a couple of boys years ago and . . ."

Chief Bicks shook his head sadly. "The swamps got both those missing boys. That's my bet. Not a shred of evidence ever implicated old man Turner. Just vicious talk, that's all it ever was."

His parents were already out the kitchen door and hurrying toward the truck. Chief Bicks winked at him. "Now you let me do the talking, Alex, and these folks of yours will figure you for a hero, not a delinquent."

They got out of the truck. His mother hugged him, and Chief Bicks began explaining. But Alex didn't feel like a hero.

# five

When his parents came upstairs to his room after supper, he was at his desk trying to repair his model of the *Constitution*, which had been demolished during moving. Its broken pieces helped to keep his mind off everything that had happened today.

"How's it going?" his father asked, sitting down on the edge of his bed.

"Okay."

His mother came over to his desk and ran her hand through his hair. They hadn't talked to him about old man Turner during supper—it was a family rule that only pleasant things were discussed at meals. So they hadn't talked much at all, and Alex had pushed his food around and then excused himself.

Now, he felt, they would want to talk to him, and he dreaded their questions.

"Alex?"

He turned in his seat and faced his father. "Yes, sir?"

"Your mother and I both realize how upset you are." His father looked tired, sitting there on Alex's bed. His pale face was lined, his shirt rumpled. Even his ordinarily lively eyes were still. Without their light, his whole face lost its strength and character and just looked ugly. Alex wondered if the long daily drives to work, the new job, the confusion of living out of boxes while they renovated the old farmhouse were making him hate the move, too.

"We really do know how you feel," his mother said. Impulsively she bent down and kissed the top of his head. "We know you would never enjoy another person's suffering."

Alex broke away from her and went to the window. It was night now, too dark to see much beyond the reflection in the glass of the room behind him; but the lower window was open, and the summer night smells of the trees and grass came through to him, strange and unfamiliar even after two weeks.

"They made him sound like a monster with all their stories," Alex told them. He again saw the look in the old man's eyes and the way his face had caved in when he had collapsed into the stream. "I was just scared he'd catch me. I wasn't hurting his pond. I wasn't even taking any fish."

"We know that, Alex," his father said. "You were never raised to bait or torment anyone, no matter how different they might appear to be."

"It's just we're very concerned about those other two," his mother broke in. "Fritz and Benny, you said their names are?"

"Yeah."

"We don't want you hanging out with them," his father said.

"I'm not going to." In the reflection in the window Alex could see his father stand up.

"That's all we want to hear," he said.

"We know it's hard for you," his mother said. "But you'll make other friends."

"I don't need friends," he told them angrily.

"Of course you do," she said. "We all do."

He turned around to face them before they could leave his room. He hated himself for crying again. "Couldn't we call?" he asked them. "Call the hospital and find out how he is?"

His mother looked at his father. "We don't have the phone yet and . . . "

"I know. But couldn't we drive to a phone booth?"

His father gave him a weary smile. "Okay, Alex. We'll drive into Letford Center. We can pick up some ice cream at the store."

His mother stayed home, and he and his father drove into Letford Center in silence. As they passed Four Corners, Alex wondered which of the two houses Fritz and Benny lived in.

While his father called, he picked out the ice cream and paid for it with the money his father had given him. Then he waited in the front of the store, looking through a rack of paperbacks.

"Let's go, Alex," his father said behind him. "Did you find any chocolate chip?"

"Yeah." By the time they reached the car, Alex couldn't contain himself any longer. "What did they say?"

His father stopped and looked down at him. "The hospital

wouldn't give out any information. So I called Chief Bicks.''

"And?''

"He said Mr. Turner was moved to the intensive care ward at Mercy Hospital in Kingston. Apparently he did have a heart attack, just as Chief Bicks suspected.''

On the drive back, Alex sat as frozen and cold as the package of ice cream he held in his lap. All he could think, over and over again, was how much he wanted old man Turner to get well, how much he wanted him to live. Because if the old man died, he and Fritz and Benny were murderers.

Fritz and Benny were waiting for him in the morning in the bushes behind his house, and the moment he came outside, they called him down. He walked reluctantly toward them, not wanting to see them, not wanting to talk, but certain that he would never run away from them.

"Here comes Mr. Big Mouth now,'' Fritz said loudly as he reached the bushes. "Here comes the new fink in town.''

He stared at them, hating them as if he'd known them all his life. Above them the sky was hung with quiet gray clouds, and a mist drifted through the trees beyond the railroad tracks. It was too quiet a day for all the violence he felt bottled up inside him.

Fritz poked him in the shoulder. "How come you had to hang around there yesterday? How come you had to spill your guts to Bicks?''

"I didn't give him your names,'' Alex told them. "He knew you were there anyway.''

Benny snorted so hard he had to wipe his face on his sleeve. "Like hell he did!''

"He did. And I didn't tell him about the rock throwing."

"That was sweet of you," Fritz said sarcastically. "Benny and me are sure glad of that."

"You should have left him there," Benny said. "Like we did. We'd be rid of him now for good."

"Alex had to be a hero," Fritz said to Benny. "Had to save him. Then he got Bicks on our case."

"Maybe we should teach him a lesson," Benny suggested.

Alex looked at Benny, then back at Fritz. He had an eerie feeling that they had rehearsed this all word for word on the walk over from their house.

"Go to hell," he told them and started to turn away. He saw the movement as Benny took a clumsy swing at his head. He ducked and brought his fist up hard into Benny's stomach. The fat boy hunched over in pain and staggered back.

But Fritz was a much better fighter than Benny, not as street wise as some of the tough boys Alex had fought in Boston, but hard and strong and totally without fear or caring. Even so, Alex held his own, until Benny knocked him to the ground and pinned him there while Fritz pounded his face.

His nose was bleeding heavily when they finally gave up the sport. Benny pushed himself up onto his feet while Fritz gave Alex a final kick in the ribs. Then they raced off toward the tracks. Alex watched them go with one eye already swelling closed. He wanted to shout after them to come back and fight him one at a time, but his rage was caught in the clot of blood in his throat.

He tried to sneak into the house without being seen, but his mother saw him before he reached the stairs.

"Alex!"

"Fell out of a tree," he mumbled and tried to duck past her, but she had his arm by then.

"Was it those two boys?"

Even with only one eye open he could see her tears plainly enough. He shook his head. "No."

"Don't lie to me!"

He stood there silently and realized that blood was again dripping from his nose. He wiped it on his sleeve.

"I'm calling Chief Bicks."

"No, Mom, don't do that. It won't help."

She stood there uncertainly, her eyes wide with concern for him.

"I'm okay, really, Mom."

"Sure you are! You look like a train ran over you!"

She took him into the kitchen and washed his face and stopped the nosebleed. But she insisted on finding a doctor to look at his black eye. She got her car out of the barn, and they rode around half the day before they finally got in to see a doctor at the emergency room in the Milton Falls Hospital.

On the way home she had calmed down enough to stop and buy lunch. She stared at him over their hamburgers and shook her head. "I don't know, Alex. This is just the kind of thing we moved out of Boston to get away from."

He didn't dare repeat his story about falling out of a tree, but he wasn't going to admit that Fritz and Benny had done this to him. He had to live in this town that his parents had chosen over Boston, he had to go to school here and find a place with the other kids. And he wasn't going to start out by acquiring a reputation as a fink.

"It'll be okay," he told his mother.

"Look at you," she said, almost crying again. "What will your father say?"

But that evening his father looked at his face and said nothing at all.

# six

Exactly when Alex first thought of going down to Kingston to see old man Turner he wasn't sure, but the idea grew day by day until he was certain it was what he should do.

He said nothing to his parents about it; he thought they would not understand. He would have been hard put to explain to them what he wanted to say to the old man. It was more than wanting to tell him he was sorry for what had happened. It had something to do with wanting to tell him he was not like the others, that he had meant him no harm, that he had only become involved in the incident at the stream by accident.

Kingston, he could tell by a map in his mother's car, was nearly fifty miles away, south on Route 17. He planned on walking to Letford Center, since the local traffic was so light, then hitching rides from there. All he needed was an excuse to be gone for the whole day.

But his mother solved this problem for him herself by deciding to drive down to Kingston to buy some wallpaper. She expected him to go with her, and once there he would only have to slip away for an hour or two.

On the day they went down the traffic was light southbound, and they made good time. His mother was in good spirits and sang as she drove. He thought it was nice to see her dressed in something besides paint-stained jeans and he told her so.

"My, what a flatterer you're becoming," she said with a laugh. And then she glanced over at him with a more serious expression on her face. "I hope Letford will turn out to be good for you, Alex. It's not Boston and I really do miss Boston, sometimes more than I admit to. But we have to give up one thing to get something else, and then we have to grow enough to be able to get all we can out of the new situation."

She laughed again and let go of the steering wheel for a moment in mock disgust. "I never was much with words," she said. "But do you understand what I'm trying to say?"

"Yes, I do." Alex felt suddenly how much he loved her. For a moment he almost decided to share with her his plan to see old man Turner today. But then she might object, and it was something he had to do no matter what.

In Kingston they parked downtown and had lunch. His mother planned on stopping in several shops to check different wallpaper designs before buying any, and he had little trouble convincing her he would only be in the way and bored besides.

"You know how I can be," he said, and she laughed. "I'd like to get some new models," he added, and she let him go.

He asked directions on the street and found the hospital at last. It turned out when he got there that he could have taken a bus a block from where they had parked the car. But at least he knew now he could save some time by going back that way. It was important his mother not have too long to wonder where he had disappeared to.

Mercy Hospital was large and full of people. Visiting hours had begun at one, and he simply blended into the traffic in the corridors, following signs as he went along and pretending he knew exactly where he was going. He'd seen his mother get into places several times just because she acted so sure of herself no one questioned her.

Unfortunately he was not an adult, and no matter how he tried to attach himself to various groups of people, he found himself alone by the time he reached the intensive care ward on the third floor. He kept right on walking, was stopped by one nurse, found out Mr. Turner was in room C4, and almost got there before he was stopped by another nurse, who sent him back to the nurses' station.

"I'm Mr. Turner's grandson," he lied, trying to sound convincing.

The nurse looked right through him. 'I'm sorry, but only immediate family can visit patients on this ward." She riffled through some papers on the desk. "Your name?"

He knew his chances with her were slim. "Randolph Turner."

The nurse looked at him again. He smiled at her.

"I'm sorry. I don't have your name here. I just can't let you in."

"I'll check with the doctor," he said to cover his retreat and turned to walk away. The moment she looked down, he slipped into a men's room.

He waited there for several long minutes, peeking out every so often, until the moment came when all the nurses were busy, leaving the station unattended. He stepped out and headed up the corridor toward room C4.

No one saw him. He projected confidence and glided along as fast as he dared, and in a minute he was through the door of room C4. There were no nurses inside. He had made it!

Mr. Turner was alone in the room, stretched out on the bed with wires attached to him running to a panel on the wall behind him. They had trimmed his beard so close to his face that at first Alex thought he had made a mistake and was in the wrong room. But then the old man seemed to sense he was there and opened his eyes.

They were the same eyes that had stared at him from the stream that afternoon with Fritz and Benny. Now again they seemed to look into him, to bore into his head. And the eyes seemed to say so much, but in a language Alex couldn't understand.

They both started to speak at the same time. The old man only managed to say, "You . . . " And Alex was cut off after saying, "Mr. Turner, I . . . "

For then the door opened and a hand grabbed him roughly by the shoulder. "What are you doing in here?"

Alex saw a tall, dark-haired man in a perfectly creased suit staring down at him. His fingers dug hard into Alex's shoulder.

"I-I'm visiting Mr. Turner," he managed to stammer.

A nurse came. "Oh, Dr. Starvos, I . . . "

"Nurse, what is this boy doing in here?"

Since the nurse didn't know, she could only become more flustered. Alex guessed that the doctor was more interested in finding fault with the nurse than in doing anything with him.

He broke away and looked quickly toward Mr. Turner before darting to the door. Was it only his imagination or did Mr. Turner give him a small wave before sinking back onto his pillow?

Alex had no time to think about it then. He ran from the room and had to dive past two other nurses before he regained the outer corridor.


His mother was sitting in the car waiting for him as he walked toward her from the bus stop. She got out and hurried over to him.

"Where have you been?" she demanded. "Do you know what time it is?"

He knew it was late. She was angry with him and he didn't feel like lying anymore.

"Where are your models?" she asked.

"I didn't get any. I went to visit Mr. Turner at the hospital."

She stared at him. Then something inside her relaxed and she smiled faintly. "I should have guessed."

As they drove out of Kingston, she asked him how the visit had gone.

He shrugged. "We didn't get a chance to talk. A doctor came in and made me leave." Alex thought about the wave Mr. Turner had given him as he left. He was sure now that it had been a wave.

"Mr. Turner had something he wanted to say to me," he told his mother. "I'm sure of it."

They headed back toward North Letford. His mother patted his knee. "Maybe when he comes home, you can ask him what it was."

# seven

As the days of July passed slowly by, Alex found himself more and more drawn to explore the area around Fog Hollow Station. Other than Fritz and Benny, North Letford seemed empty of kids; in his wanderings he met no one else.

He did occasionally see Fritz and Benny in the distance, usually near the tracks. Since it was their established territory, he couldn't expect them to abandon it, so he stayed away from them as much as he could. The afternoon he stumbled onto their secret swimming hole, they made it very clear that they still hated him for rescuing old man Turner.

It was a hot afternoon in mid-July, and he decided to follow the tracks awhile to see what they led to. He crossed the trestle and walked slowly past Fog Hollow Station, hoping, yet also fearing, that old man Turner had returned. But the station lay still and brooding in the blazing sun, the padlock Chief Bicks had placed on the front door still barring entrance to the dark, mysterious rooms inside.

Beyond the station the stream that ran from the fishing pond through the woods, crossing the tracks beneath the trestle, reemerged from the swamp grass and the maples, already turning red in the middle of summer, to run beside the tracks. Heading south as he was, too, it kept him company for over a mile, running slowly on the right-hand side of the tracks, gurgling over occasional rocks, silent elsewhere in the heavy heat of the day. Frogs plopped into its shallow pools as he walked by, and red-winged blackbirds flew away and came back and watched him.

He came at last to a high grove of trees where the stream disappeared into green, cool woods. A path led down from the tracks into the grove, and he followed it without thinking, lured on by the promise of cool shade. He heard splashing and laughter, and suddenly he came out of the trees onto a grassy bank above a small, roughly oval pool formed by a wide place in the stream that had been dammed with sand bags at the far end. Down near the sand bags he saw Fritz and Benny swimming. Beyond them under a huge spruce tree was a crude hut of old boards and rusty steel roofing.

He tried to leave as he had come, but Benny spotted him.

"Hey, Fritz," he shouted. "The fink's here."

Fritz climbed out of the water and pulled on a pair of tattered cutoffs. He glanced several times in Alex's direction and shouted at Benny to hurry up and get dressed. But Benny seemed reluctant to leave the privacy of the water.

Alex stood his ground. To leave now would make them think he was afraid of them, and that would be one more black mark against him.

Fritz walked along the bank toward him. Without Benny, who still stood half-submerged in the pool, Fritz seemed smaller, less menacing. But still his fists were tightly clenched.

"You ain't welcome here, fink," he said.

Alex looked around at the trees that shaded the pool and nearly covered the sky with their high, green leaves.

"It's nice here," was all he said. He turned to go. He walked very slowly away, without looking back, to let Fritz know he wasn't afraid of him.

Fritz began shouting at him as he walked away. "You stay out of here, fink! You come back here and we'll teach you a worse lesson than before. We got booby traps rigged all around these woods."

His voice rose higher and higher as Alex walked away. He bounced partway along the path in his bare feet. "You don't belong here," he screamed. "Go back where you came from."

Alex sometimes went to fish alone in the pond behind Fog Hollow Station. Fritz and Benny didn't seem to come there now that old man Turner was gone. Alex explored the woods around the pond and waded through the swamp on its south side. He found a flat rock where he could sit and fish in the shade most of the afternoon and a dewy little cove where the mornings were lit by a special green light.

He often thought of Boston and of his old friend Charlie, while he sat there waiting for the fish to bite, and wished that

Charlie could be with him here. But Charlie had only written once and had not answered his invitation to visit. His letter had seemed distant and uninterested.

Alex caught only sunfish and threw them all back. Occasionally though, in the mornings, he would see larger fish out in the middle of the pond jumping for bugs, and he wondered if they were trout.

Sometimes he felt so much a stranger here in this strange country, and he longed with all his heart to know it better and to belong. He would remember how Fritz had screamed at him by the secret swimming hole, had told him to get out, had told him he didn't belong here.

It hurt because he felt it was true.

Each night in his room when the nightly freight train roared by, whistling for the crossings, he imagined that its voice spoke the loneliness he felt and wailed it across the countryside as he would never dare. For he would talk of this with no one.

One morning he fished nearly until noon, until it was obvious the fish were hiding deep in the cool water and weren't going to be lured by his worms. He headed back along the path, and then on the tracks he heard a car close by.

Looking around, he saw a cloud of dust beyond the trees down toward Fog Hollow Station. It took him a moment to realize someone was driving down the dirt lane that ran from the road to the station. At once he thought that old man Turner was coming home, and he hurried to hide his fishing pole in the woods. Then he walked slowly along the tracks toward the station, hoping it would be the old man, yet fearful, too.

Perhaps he had been wrong in the hospital, perhaps the old man hadn't waved to him as he ran out. Perhaps the old man only saw him as another Fritz or Benny, a hated enemy, a thrower of rocks. . . .

Alex saw an old black Ford sedan parked near the tracks. As he crept closer, he saw that the front door of the station was still locked, but he could hear sounds from inside. He walked around and mounted the back steps. The door was ajar, the padlock unlocked. He rapped softly on the edge of the doorway, then in silence, rapped again.

"Hooligan!"

Alex jumped back, but not before a heavy hand slapped him hard on the side of his face. He fell down the steps and looked up into the enraged face of a stout woman with frizzy gray hair who stood in the doorway above him.

"Hooligan!" she shouted again. "It's not enough you gave my brother a heart attack, now you're back for more! Plague an old man, give him no peace. I'll show you what you deserve!"

She came heavily down the steps, swinging a stick in one hand. Alex scrambled to his feet and backed away.

"I didn't come to bother him," he shouted as she followed him out into the gravel yard behind the station. "I only wanted . . ."

"To what?" she demanded, stopping a few feet away, still brandishing the stick, perspiration running down her angry red face.

"Is he okay?" Alex managed to ask her .

She nodded slowly. "But no thanks to the likes of you."

"Will he be coming home?"

"He's going to stay with me. I'm here to fetch some of his things. He needs to get his strength back." She waved one hand at the station. "If I have anything to say about it, he'll never return to this hell on earth."

"Will you tell your brother something for me?" Alex asked.

She looked at him for several moments, as if for the first time she was seeing him as an individual. "You *are* one of those boys who . . ." she started to ask.

Alex shook his head. "I was only there." He took a deep breath. "Will you tell him I'm sorry?"

Slowly she nodded.

They stood there for a moment regarding each other in the still, hot afternoon.

"I'll tell him," she said at last.

# eight

Alex waited all summer for old man Turner to return. The swamp maples turned scarlet beside the pond, and the air on chilly August mornings had a flavor that told of summer's end. One morning in the cool hush at the pond he looked up from baiting his hook and saw a narrow column of wood smoke rising above the trees from the direction of Fog Hollow Station. He knew then that the hermit had come home.

A strange shyness took hold of him and try as he would, he could not bring himself to go to the station. The smoke faded as the day grew warm, but the next morning, it was there again, like a signal fire calling him to come, and yet he couldn't.

"Old man Turner is back," he told his parents the first night, but to their questions he had nothing to add, because he hadn't seen him face to face or exchanged a word with him.

On several mornings at the pond Alex had a strong feeling someone was watching him. He would look around expecting the old man's eyes to be upon him, but if they were, it was from the shelter of some hiding place in the woods and no rustle in the branches betrayed him.

Yet the feeling of being watched grew stronger with each passing day, as summer changed slowly to autumn, as the green leaves became the yellows and reds of fall and the wind shifted from warm breezes to chilly gusts. School would be starting soon, his free and lonely summer would be over, and the old hermit would remain a mystery. And yet he was afraid to make the first move.

Then one morning the old man stepped out of the woods as Alex approached the pond on the path from the railroad tracks. Turner stepped out of the shadows into the path directly before him and stood there, not twenty feet away. Alex's throat went dry.

The old man was again wearing overalls and a plaid shirt, and his white beard had begun to grow long again. He was much thinner now, except for his face, which had a puffy, unhealthy look around the eyes.

But his eyes still blazed like search beams.

"Why did you come to the hospital?" he asked Alex. His voice was deep and gruff, but the words came slowly, as if each one had been separately chosen, held up to view, put carefully in place like rocks in a stone wall.

Alex took a deep breath. "To tell you I was sorry about what happened here." Alex looked around. They were standing just a few feet from the place in the stream where the old man had collapsed. "Didn't your sister tell you?"

The old man nodded. "She did."

None of the things that Alex had thought to say to him if he ever got the chance came to mind now. They stood looking at each other for a long, silent time, then the old man grunted.

"You're wasting your time fishing here," he said, the words coming so slowly, so heavily.

Alex misunderstood and turned to leave.

"Wait."

Alex turned back, but the old man was gone.

"Wait," came his voice from the woods.

When old man Turner returned, Alex was standing by the edge of the pond, gazing out over its wind-ruffled surface. The old man held a fishing pole of his own and a small tackle box.

"We'll go up to High Meadow," the old man told him. "There are fish up there that never tasted hooks."

They traveled from path to path, starting on the hillside beyond the pond where Alex had fished all summer. But soon the old man was leading the way through a dark pine forest where no paths disturbed the perfect carpet of brown needles. Then they angled across the back side of a small mountain, crossed several streams, and worked their way under the brow of a high, granite cliff to come out at last onto meadowland where the tall, uncut grass rippled in the wind like waves at sea.

Alex, expecting the sun to be on his right, was surprised to find it on his left and realized he had somehow got completely turned around.

"Where are we?" he asked.

For the first time the old man smiled. He was breathing hard and there was sweat beaded over his entire face, but the flash of his strong teeth gave Alex for a moment a sense of the younger man he had once been. Even when he sank down upon a boulder and grimaced in pain, rubbing at his chest as if to make the pain disappear, Alex still thought there was something about him too childlike to be old.

"We'll rest here a moment," the old man gasped. He took out a pillbox and slipped a small tablet into his mouth.

"Maybe we shouldn't have come," Alex said. But the old man shook his head.

"Stay in my bed so that I can be comfortable when I die?" he growled. The pain was gradually leaving his face. "I'd rather die out here, with the sky over me, not a sheet."

Alex remembered how frightened the old man had looked that first afternoon when he had returned to the stream with Chief Bicks and the ambulance crew. He wondered what had changed the old man's fear to this gruff acceptance of his bad heart.

As if reading Alex's thoughts, the old man stared at him with his steady eyes. "Death is just an idea that takes you time to get used to. Then you're not so afraid. It's a nasty surprise when first it comes at you, but then you make friends with it."

Although his words came slowly, his thoughts seemed sharp and clear. Alex realized suddenly that the slowness of speech must be the result of living alone for so long that talking was no longer natural. And so each word was spoken carefully, and the result was this strange sense of lag, of a mind racing ahead of its voice.

He looked around him at the acres of field ringed by distant trees. He caught glimpses of a pond through the yellow grass.

"Where are we?" he asked again.

The old man put away his pills and stood up. "High Meadow," he said. "It's not so far away from everything as it seems. But no one comes here anymore."

He led the way across the field to the pond. A few trees bordered it, and at one end a stream came tumbling into it from a rocky arm of the woods. There was a rowboat hidden under some bushes, and Alex helped the old man pull it out and turn it right side up.

"Carried this here myself, years ago," the old man said, now wiping the sweat from his eyes. "Can you row?"

"A little."

The old man laughed roughly. "A little is all we need."

They fished for a couple of hours, drifting on the pond as the wind took them, bailing out the water that leaked in. The old man showed Alex where to cast his line and gave him a spinner to use. They shared the worms Alex carried in a small box filled with grass that he changed every day.

"Row us up closer to the stream," old man Turner told Alex. "The water's colder there." And when they were there, he pointed to a large, moss-covered boulder that jutted out from the bank. "Cast over by that boulder and troll back slowly."

Alex did as he was told, felt some tentative nibbles, then a harder tug, and he immediately yanked on his line to set the hook. He saw a flash of iridescent green in the water.

"Brook trout," the old man called to him from the other end of the boat. "Big one, too. Easy does it!"

Alex had never landed a trout before, and his heart was pounding with joy by the time the fish was safely in the boat.

He removed the hook carefully and put the trout into the plastic bag he had been carrying around all summer.

"Must be near a pound," the old man said. "Give it a rap on the head against the side of the boat. No need for it to suffer."

Later Alex brought in a small brook trout, and the old man caught one but lost it. By noon the fish were nodding in the depths of the pond, and they let their lines drift, not expecting any more strikes. Alex felt happier than he'd felt all summer. To be here on this pond at High Meadow, so remote and lonely a spot, was a thrill in itself. But to be sharing it with the old man made his heart want to sing.

"You've not told me your name," the old man said.

"Alex. Alex Webb."

He stuck out his hand. Alex took it and felt the rough power of it around his. "Then we're friends," the old man said. "And you can call me Mr. Turner, or old man Turner, whichever pleases you."

Alex nodded. "Mr. Turner, thanks for bringing me here."

The old man looked away at the grass waving in the breeze. "Well, there was no sense in your wasting any more time on those sunfish."

They reeled in their lines and the old man brought out two apples, handing one to Alex. It was tart and green but flavorful.

"The first ones this year," the old man said. "There are a couple of apple trees in a field behind the station."

Alex leaned back in his end of the boat and watched the clouds drift by overhead.

"See the wispy ones, high above the little puffs of cumulus?"

Alex nodded. He studied the faint web of clouds that stretched halfway across the sky.

"Cirrus," the old man told him. "A mackerel sky. Means rain by tomorrow."

"How do you know?"

"There's always a series to events," the old man told him. "You learn to read the signs after a while."

"Then you can tell what the future will bring?" Alex asked.

"Sometimes." The old man's voice was low and gruff again. "Sometimes I can."

Later, on the way home, old man Turner took a detour around one end of the meadow and showed him some cellar holes.

"People lived here one hundred and fifty years ago, Alex. This one here belonged to a family named Burke. They had two children go insane; the youngest boy, he burned them out of the house."

They wandered through the little settlement of cellar holes, nearly overtaken now by the growth of trees and vines. "This one was for the parsonage, near as I can figure. And over there was a root cellar in a small cave."

"They had a pretty place to live," Alex said, looking back toward the meadow through the trees.

"They did. A fine place. Back then people pushed off into the wilderness to find their own little worlds. Didn't clump together like vermin, the way they do now."

On the return walk through the woods in the windy afternoon, Alex tried to memorize landmarks to help guide him back there someday. They had to stop once for old man Turner to rest and take another of his pills, and when they reached the old familiar pond near the tracks, he looked suddenly gray and weary.

"I'll leave you here," he said abruptly and walked away toward Fog Hollow Station. Alex watched him go from sight, and then headed for the tracks. He clutched his pole and the bag containing his two wonderful trout, but somehow now their magic was gone.

Overhead the clouds had formed a milky ceiling in the sky, and the next day, sure enough, it rained.

# nine

School began the following week, and Alex, caught up in the newness of it all, was swept away from the beginnings of his friendship with old man Turner. He was starting junior high with classmates who knew each other but not him, in a school system that seemed strange and alien compared to the schools he was used to. There was a rawness here that startled him; there were none of the separate niches that he'd known in bigger schools. And being an outsider, he sometimes felt as though he'd been thrown into deep water and told to swim or drown.

His class was made up of kids from several sixth grades, but he was the only one to come in without any allies. Fritz was the only one he knew from the start, and before the first two days had gone by, Fritz had managed to get to every boy he knew and tell his lies. Alex was challenged twice, once in gym and once on the bus, and by Friday he had already been called into the principal's office for fighting.

"I'm hoping you're going to make an effort to fit in here," the principal told him, and Alex wanted to tell him not to count on it, but he was too polite to say this. Instead he nodded and said he would try.

He told his parents none of this. It would have been too easy to blame them for it all since they had wanted to move here and he hadn't. So he kept still and spent the weekend helping his father tear out a wall in what would someday be their dining room.

But each night the freight train going by behind the house reminded him of old man Turner living alone at Fog Hollow Station, and he felt a kinship with him and wondered how he was.

In the middle of September he visited the old man on a rainy afternoon after school. His shyness persisted even though they had spent most of a day fishing together, and his doubts followed him as he walked in the rain along the tracks toward Fog Hollow station. Perhaps the old man didn't really want him for a friend. Perhaps taking him fishing at High Meadow had been a fluke, brought on by his being weak and sick. Perhaps the old man would chase him away. . . .

Smoke drifted wetly from the chimney of the station, but no light showed through the windows into the gloomy afternoon. Alex walked around back and knocked on the door. A mist hung over the trees in the swamp behind the station.

He knocked several times before the door opened. And then the old man stood there without saying a word. The scent of wood smoke rushed out of the doorway around him.

"I wondered how you were," Alex managed to say at last.

The old man's eyes did not even seem to blink. "Did you now."

Alex nodded, his heart sinking heavily. The old man's coldness hit him like a physical blow.

"Come in out of the rain," the old man said at last.

Inside the kitchen the stove sputtered but threw a good heat. A large book lay open on the table by the window. The old man lit a kerosene lamp and then regarded him in its flickering light. Behind him Alex watched the rain running down the dirty glass.

"I thought maybe our fishing trip to High Meadow wasn't exciting enough for you."

Alex tried to understand what he was saying. It didn't make sense.

The old man put the lamp down on the table. "Well, you've come and seen that I'm all right. Nothing's keeping you."

Alex looked toward the door. "Do you want me to go?"

"Why should I care what you do?" the old man said angrily. His face swung around toward Alex, and his words seemed to be thrown at him one by one. "Do you think I spend any time caring what you or other people do?"

Alex recognized something in his anger. "I started school. It's not going very well. I wanted to come by but . . ."

"You don't need to make excuses," the old man shouted.

"I'm not!" Alex started for the door, but the old man grabbed his arm. Alex pulled away and looked at him. "You're feeling sorry for yourself," he said and then couldn't believe he'd said it.

"And what makes you think you can be so honest with me?" the old man asked.

Alex hesitated. "I don't know."

In the silence that followed Alex heard the rain driving against the window. Little light came through the window, even less from the kerosene lamp. When the old man opened the stove to throw in more wood, the flames bathed them both in a red glow.

"Have a cup of tea before you go back out into the rain," the old man told him. He moved the teapot over the fire and set out a cup without waiting to see if Alex agreed.

The tea was bitter and the old man had no sugar. Alex forced himself to drink it anyway.

"What are you reading?" he asked, looking toward the book on the table, trying to fill the silence.

"*Walden,*" the old man said. "Thoreau. I've read it before, but I'm finding new meanings." The old man refilled his cup. "Have you read it?"

Alex shook his head.

"Go ahead, look at it."

Alex glanced through several pages but found the long paragraphs intimidating and the heavy prose even more formidable. He shook his head and looked up to find the old man watching him.

"I can't understand it."

The old man snorted. "It's not that hard. What grade of school are you in?"

"Seventh."

"Time enough then to turn away from fairy tales and begin reading true things. Give it here."

Alex lifted the heavy volume and handed it to him. The old man leafed through the pages, then read a passage aloud:

"I have a great deal of company in my house; especially in the morning, when nobody calls. Let me suggest a few comparisons, that some one may convey an idea of my situation. I am no more lonely than the loon in the pond that laughs so loud, or than Walden Pond itself. What company has that lonely lake, I pray? And yet it has not the blue devils, but the blue angels in it, in the azure tint of its waters. The sun is alone, except in thick weather, when there sometimes appear to be two, but one is a mock sun. God is alone,—but the devil, he is far from being alone; he sees a great deal of company; he is legion. I am no more lonely than a single mullein or dandelion in a pasture, or a bean leaf, or sorrel, or a horse-fly, or a humble-bee. I am no more lonely than the Mill Brook, or a weathercock, or the north star, or the south wind, or an April shower, or a January thaw, or the first spider in a new house."

The old man put the book down in his lap. "Well, tell me what that means?" he asked.

The sentences spoken aloud had come to life in Alex's mind, as if they were fresh thoughts, not old, dead words in an old, dead book. "He's talking about people like you," he said in a low voice. "People who live alone." Alex looked away and then back at the old man, whose gaze never wavered. "He's saying that you're not alone any more than the pond or the plants or the insects are alone. I guess he means you're part of nature, the way they are."

Alex felt as though he were being tested and didn't know why, but somehow he sensed it was very important not to fail this test.

"I didn't understand the part about the blue devils," he added.

The rain poured down harder against the window. The old man grunted. He stood up and rummaged behind a chair until he found a heavy grocery bag large enough for the book. "Here," he said. "Take this home and read what you can. I have another copy around here somewhere. It will give us something to talk about."

Outside, the rain closed in around Alex, and he tried to pretend he was a bubble. He clutched the book in its brown bag close to his chest to protect it. Halfway to the trestle he turned to look back at the station and thought he saw the old man watching him from the window. But it was too far to be sure.

# ten

Alex read most of Thoreau's *Walden* during the next few weeks, skipping pages when the sentences got too entangled for him, rereading the parts that he only half understood. He liked best the parts in which Thoreau told directly of his experiences during his two-year stay in his cabin beside Walden Pond: the bean field, the descriptions of winter, the other very real and concrete images. The philosophy for the most part eluded him.

Old man Turner would growl at him when he confessed this. "You've got to learn to read with your mind, not just your heart," he said. "Poetry's fine, but not without the thought behind it."

Alex came to see him two or three times a week, and they

would argue about the book and drink tea and argue some more. Gradually Alex realized that the old man relished their most violent disagreements. He didn't want Alex to agree with him; he wanted something else. . . .

"But the part about having to read the classics in their original language, that's dumb," Alex protested late one afternoon when he was having trouble tearing himself away to go home.

Old man Turner smacked the copy of *Walden* on his knee with his open hand. "Why?" he demanded. "Because that useless school you go to won't teach Greek or Latin anymore?"

"Because I don't want to learn Greek or Latin. There isn't time to learn everything."

The old man's face broke into a triumphant smile. "Yes, Alex, but how do you know what's important to learn and what's not?"

Alex shrugged. "By what people tell me and . . ."

"Right!" old man Turner broke in. "And Thoreau, who was very well educated and brilliant besides, is telling you that the classics in their original languages are important."

"But it sounds like he's being such a snob, just because he can read Greek and the rest of us have trouble enough with English."

The old man laughed. "Perhaps."

"Anyway, I still like the bean field and the weather and the pond and the animals best."

Old man Turner nodded slowly. "So do I, Alex. And the end of the book, when you reach it, you'll see it's the best of all."

When he got home that night, Alex was late for supper. His father angrily bawled him out, and later his mother came up to his room where he was again racing through his homework in order to tackle *Walden*.

She flipped through the pages of the large book resting on one corner of his desk. "You spend a lot of time on this lately," she said. "You mustn't neglect your other studies."

"I'm not. It's just that they seem so dumb compared to . . . to this."

"Your father is concerned about the amount of time you're spending with the old man." His mother looked worried too. "He feels it's not healthy."

"Why?" Alex asked. A cold fear crept over him, a fear that they would somehow take his new friend away from him.

"We'd like to see you playing with boys your own age," his mother said.

Alex said nothing. The hostility from the other boys at school was still his secret. What Fritz had started with his lies had been continued and increased by the fights Alex had had with several of his classmates. Any chance he might have had to blend in smoothly had been lost from the start, and his reputation as a troublemaking outsider followed him from day to day.

"We just want you to know how we feel," his mother said at last. "We've hardly ever told you with whom you should be friends and with whom you shouldn't, but . . ."

Alex clenched his pencil. "But what?"

"Just think about what's best for you. I'm sure the old man is very nice, but he can hardly take the place of a boy or two your own age who . . ."

"I like him."

"Yes, I know, Alex. But how much fun can he be to be around?"

"He isn't fun."

"Then . . ."

Alex whirled around in his chair to face her. "He isn't fun. He's a whole lot more than that. He's real and he's smart and he . . .he . . ."

"What, Alex?"

"He knows things. He's seen things." Alex looked into his mother's face, hoping to read understanding there but not seeing any. "He isn't like anyone else I've ever known."

When his mother left his room, he slammed his schoolwork into his notebook and pulled *Walden* over into the light from his desk lamp. Soon he was back at Walden Pond deep in the snows of a long-ago winter.

The ending of *Walden* went off in his head like a bomb, for there seemed to be so much more there than the paragraphs or pages could hold. He hurried to Fog Hollow Station the next afternoon after school and found the old man resting on his chopping block, the split wood scattered all around him. His face was red, almost purple, but he laughed with Alex over his excitement. The October wind tried to snatch away their words.

"You were right," Alex said. "The whole ending seems to blow up in your face as you read it."

The old man nodded. "And do you think it's partly the difficulties beforehand that make the brilliance of the ending so much of a discovery?"

Alex began picking up firewood. "I think so," he said. "It

was like coming up out of the sea into the light.'' He carried in one armload of wood, then came out for another. ''And I read something I'd heard somewhere before.''

'' 'If a man does not keep pace with his companions,' '' the old man recited from memory, '' 'perhaps it is because he hears a different drummer. Let him step to the music which he hears, however measured or far away.' ''

Alex nodded. ''How did you know?''

The old man laughed. ''It's the one bit of Thoreau that everyone has heard. But do you understand it?''

''Sure.''

''Yes?''

Alex felt suddenly self-conscious. The wind was blowing chips of wood around the yard. The old man was watching him as he bent down for more wood.

''If you're different from other people around you,'' Alex began.

''Yes?''

''Maybe it's because you know something other people don't know, and you should follow this and not give it up just because it's different or hard to understand or other people say you're crazy, they don't understand what you see or hear or feel.'' Alex finished, out of breath, and bent to the wood. When he straightened up, the old man was nodding.

''And did it mean something to you alone?'' he asked.

''Yes,'' Alex said.

They went inside and closed the back door against the wind. While making tea the old man suddenly staggered against a chair.

''It's all right,'' he growled when Alex stood up. ''Fetch my medicine. It's in the pocket of my coat.''

Alex brought him the pillbox, and the old man opened it with trembling hands. In a few minutes the pain seemed to ease and the tea preparations went on.

But their conversation the rest of that afternoon was quiet and restrained, as if the old man was listening to something else.

Before he left, Alex split some more firewood and piled it beside the old man's door.

He met Fritz and Benny on the tracks as he walked home. They were carrying some boards they had found or stolen and ignored him as he went by. But soon after, he realized they had stashed their boards and were following him. A rock whizzed by his head. He turned around to look at them, but they stopped too and waited until he resumed walking.

"Hey, finko," Benny shouted. "Old man Turner's crazy and so are you."

Alex walked on without turning again, even when another rock struck him between his shoulders.

"Gonna be a hermit when you grow up?" Fritz taunted. "Gonna be weird?"

"Hell, no," Benny shouted. "He already is!" Their laughter, tattered by the wind, followed him all the way home.

On Friday when Alex stopped by to see the old man, he found him lying on his battered sofa in the front room. He had not answered Alex's knock on the back door, and Alex had crept inside, expecting the worst. In the gloom of the front room Alex could barely see the old man stretched out on the cushions.

"Mr. Turner, are you all right?" he asked.

"Stoke up the stove," the old man told him. His words seemed separately torn from his lips, each with its own pain. "Go on. I'll be out there in a minute."

Alex went back to the kitchen and rekindled the fire in the wood stove with small pieces of the driest wood. Once it was snapping away again, he went outside after more wood. The October afternoon was rapidly cooling off as the sun sank toward the southwest. Alex buttoned his extra shirt and built up an armload of wood.

The old man was sitting at the table when he came back inside. His face was gray, and the heavy lines around his eyes and on his forehead seemed bitten in more deeply than before.

"Never see the snows this winter," the old man said softly, as if to himself or to someone else Alex couldn't see. Then he looked toward Alex and watched him throw wood on the fire.

"Alex."

"Yeah?" Alex kept his eyes on the flames.

"There's something I want to go fetch," the old man said slowly. "Something I never thought I'd want to set eyes on again. But I do, now, before it's too late."

Alex said nothing. He kept his back toward the old man, his face toward the fire.

"That's enough wood, Alex."

Alex closed the lid of the stove and shut the damper partway as he had seen the old man do.

"Will you help me?" the old man asked.

"Do what?" Alex forced himself to turn around, but something in the old man's voice frightened him so much he couldn't look into his eyes.

"Go after something I left behind years ago. I'll need your help."

"Okay."

The old man asked him to make some tea. Outside the afternoon light was fading.

"We'll go tomorrow," the old man said. "You're off from school?"

Alex nodded. "Tomorrow's Saturday."

"We'll go tomorrow," the old man repeated.

# eleven

Saturday was an Indian summer day, starting out chilly but gradually warming into a hazy, smoky afternoon. Alex had chores to do all morning and did not finally make his escape until after lunch, by which time he was sure old man Turner had left on his errand without him.

Alex hardly noticed the brilliantly colored trees as he hurried along the tracks. He had no idea what was on the old man's mind, but he had felt the urgency of it yesterday. It was important, or the old man would never have asked for his help.

Old man Turner hailed him from behind the station. "Wait there," he called. "I'll be around in a minute."

When he joined Alex on the tracks, he was wearing a stout pair of boots that laced up to his knees, as if he expected to walk a long, long way. Despite the now warm temperature, he had a heavy jacket over his plaid shirt.

"How far are we going?" Alex asked, looking down at his sneakers with their holes that showed his socks.

Old man Turner grunted vaguely and started along the ties. "When I was younger," he said, "I could do thirty miles a day without a thought of it."

Alex's heart sank, but he hurried to catch up. "Sorry I'm late," he mumbled.

The old man was holding himself stiffly erect as he walked, making his stride a kind of march that Alex found himself unconsciously copying. When he realized what he was doing, he had an eerie feeling they were going off to war.

"If we start out late," the old man growled, "we'll finish late."

Alex could have excused himself and run home, but he could not bring himself to abandon the old man. So in this sense he knew he was making his own choice: Whatever trouble he got into this afternoon, he would have no one to blame but himself. As if he were leaving home forever, he shook off all his doubts and matched his pace to the old man's.

"Where are we going?" he asked.

"You'll soon enough see."

They walked along the tracks for miles. At several crossings they could have taken roads moving off at right angles to their course, but the old man showed no interest in leaving the tracks. The warm October day grew hazy with the smoke of many distant fires, and late in the afternoon the sun came through a high overcast, which diffused its light into an angry glow that seemed to set the world itself in flames.

"When I was younger, I used to walk my demons out on these tracks," the old man said. "I'd walk all day, all night if need be."

"What demons?" Alex asked. His legs were beginning to feel the miles they'd come.

"Private ghosts," the old man told him as if that explained everything. "As familiar as friends." The old man snorted. "As treacherous, too."

Alex knew the old man was having trouble maintaining so fast a pace, but he would not stop. Twice Alex saw him slip pills into his mouth. In the livid glow of the sunset sky, his face looked even more red and swollen than it did usually. He staggered once, but straightened up and continued on.

When they finally abandoned the tracks and made their way into a spider's web of narrow streets, Alex had no idea where they were. There was nothing familiar in the look of the run-down, two-family homes that lined the street, nor of the intersections that they occasionally passed where gas stations crisscrossed the evening dark with neon reds and whites.

The old man paused across from a boarded-up church that a peeling signboard announced had once been the West Milton Falls Community Church. He grunted as if he recognized it, and they crossed the street onto a narrow back way that skirted the old burial ground behind the church. Only a low evening light lingered under the trees, and fallen yellow leaves rustled to their steps.

The old man entered the burial ground through a narrow, rusty gate that squeaked in protest. He visited three graves, but how he found the right ones in the tangle of neglect and weeds, Alex couldn't guess. The letters on the stones were too small to read in the dim light.

At the last grave, the old man paused the longest. Dogs in the distance fought loudly, then stopped as someone shouted. The old man stood like a marble shadow before this last grave. Night came finally, totally, and still he did not move away.

"Mr. Turner?" Alex asked at last.

"Ah, yes," the old man said. "You're right, Alex. We did not come this long way just to visit with the dead."

They left the burial ground and traced a tortuous, confusing course through the poor streets. Alex sensed the curious eyes that followed them through the pools of dim streetlights, but no one challenged them or asked their business here.

When the old man stopped again, it was beside a hedge that ran the length of a yard behind a house that once had been a mansion. The curved driveway still remained, as did sheds that had once been servants' quarters. But from the lights and the sounds, Alex could tell that the old mansion now housed several apartments.

"Between the hedge here and the maple tree," the old man said. "Go on, Alex, and see if there's a shovel we can use in one of the sheds."

"What?"

"A shovel. Go on, boy."

"Someone will see me."

"Not if you're quiet. Stay in the shadows."

A hundred protests crossed Alex's mind, but still he pushed through the hedge where the old man showed him the way and crept to the first shed. He knew that ordinary rules did not apply tonight; that once begun, this adventure had to be followed to the end no matter where it led.

The first shed was empty, the second locked. In the third,

against one wall, he found a rake, then a battered, heavy shovel. When he picked it up, the rake fell over.

He froze. A dog barked close by, then stopped. The ordinary noises from the apartment building continued.

When he returned to the hedge, the old man was pacing out a spot under the maple tree. "Here," he whispered loudly. "Start digging here."

Alex tried to read his face for reassurance, but in the dark no look could pass between them. It began to rain—light, misty drops. While the old man watched, he started to dig, slowly, as quietly as possible. Beyond them, yet so close Alex felt as if he could reach out and rap on any window, the old apartment building banged, laughed, and sang with the sounds of its Saturday night.

The old man had miscalculated the spot, and it took three holes to find what they had come for. Fortunately it was not buried deep and came out easily enough: a large, steel cash box, rusty with age and covered with wet earth.

The old man tried the padlock and grunted with satisfaction. "No one has touched it," he whispered. "Good work, Alex. Now fill in the holes and let's be gone from here."

The rain was coming down harder now and they were getting wet. As he was filling in the second hole, one of the back doors of the apartment building opened and a large dog bounded across the yard toward them. Alex clutched his shovel tightly, but the old man stepped forward and held out one of his hands toward the dog.

The dog backed away, then circled around them, sniffing loudly. He found the old man's hand acceptable, and Alex was able to finish filling in the holes. But before he could replace the shovel, a light flashed on and someone began calling the dog.

"Leave it!" the old man told him and pulled him through the hedge. They hurried through the streets while the owner still loudly called his dog, and the dog itself followed them for several blocks before it lost interest and circled away.

When they were a safe distance away, the old man sank down onto a bench in front of a corner grocery store and tried to catch his breath. Alex could almost feel the old man's battered heart rapping away desperately beneath his chest.

"Can I get you something in there?" Alex asked.

The old man waved away his suggestion. "They have nothing in there that will help me."

The rain continued gently, and the wet streets reflected the lights of the storefronts, giving the mean neighborhood a cover of magic in the night. Alex watched occasional cars splash by and tried to breathe for the old man, tried to lend him the steady beat of his own heart. He felt the old man's need to get back to Fog Hollow Station. Turning, he saw how the old man clutched the steel box they had just dug from its resting place in the ground.

"We can take our time, Mr. Turner," he said. "We've got all night to get home."

The old man nodded. Around them the dirty streets gleamed in the rain, and the wind began to blow, sighing in the autumn trees above them.

# twelve

After a long rest and two of his pills, the old man felt well enough to start for home. As they headed back toward the tracks, the rain stopped, and soon after that the wind blew the clouds away and the air turned cold, smelling of the north, of the arctic snows, of the ice fields beyond Canada. They hurried along, trying to keep warm inside their wet clothes. One by one the stars came out and glittered above them in the sea of the wind.

"Even if you were lost," the old man told him, "you could tell you were going north by the Pole Star up ahead."

"Which one?" Alex asked.

"Find the Big Dipper and take a line of sight from the two stars that form the far edge of the dipper. That leads you right to Polaris, the Pole Star."

With a little searching, Alex found the proper star, brighter than its nearest neighbors, a little more than halfway up the sky.

"You can always find your way by it," the old man said. "It points the way north, and it's the one star in the sky that holds its position."

The old man pointed out several of the constellations as they followed the railroad tracks toward home. Alex discovered that with the Pole Star as a reference point, he was able to find most of the star groupings the old man spoke of. For the first time in his life the stars seemed less remote, a little more familiar, a little more like friends. He stared up so long, his neck grew stiff and he tripped several times on the ties.

"Can I carry the box for you?" he asked. After a moment's hesitation, the old man handed it to him. Alex was surprised how light it was.

"I thought it was full of money," he confessed.

The old man laughed.

"What's in it?"

"Pieces of the past," the old man told him. "Things I wanted to rid myself of years ago because they hurt too much to keep, but I found it hurt too much to burn them, too. So I buried them there where I knew I could retrieve them if I ever wanted to. I never thought I'd go back after them, but . . . ."

Alex waited for him to finish, but he never did.

The far-off whistle of the night freight gave sudden size to the night. They walked on as the train slowly came closer, sounding its horn at every crossing behind them, closer, closer, until the rumble of its engine came low to them between the blasts of its horn. At last they stepped aside and watched it roar past them, a dragon in the night, a visitor from far away that had no time to stop for them.

"I crossed the country once on freights like that," the old man told him when they were back on the tracks.

Alex watched the last light of the train disappear around the bend ahead. "You did?" He tried to imagine what it would be like to cross the whole country on a bellowing beast like that.

"Yes. The country was much poorer then, back in the Depression. There were a lot of us who rode the rails looking for work, because there was no other way for us to go. We didn't think of it then as a kind of exploration, we were too desperate. But now, I remember the good things better than the bad—the people I met, the towns I saw, the mountains and the rivers and the size, the God-awful size of it all. We were a bigger country then, despite the poverty. There was more room to get lost in, maybe to find yourself in."

The old man took a deep breath as if the weight of the years was bearing down on him like the train that had just rushed by. "There were bad things too, hunger and fights and death in nameless places. But it's funny how time makes the bad things grow dim and the good memories more sharp and clear." He paused as the last whistle of the train drifted back to them on the wind. "I'm glad I went. I'm glad I saw the things I saw."

Fog Hollow Station lay like a black shadow under the stars when finally they reached it. Inside, the old man lit the kerosene lamp and Alex built a fire in the stove.

"It's after two," the old man said, consulting the alarm

clock that ticked away on the shelf above the stove. "I hope you won't be in trouble with your folks."

Alex shrugged. He was afraid of what he had to face at home, but he didn't want to make the old man feel it was his fault.

The old man's feet had swelled so badly, Alex had to help him cut his way out of his boots. The sight of his swollen ankles frightened Alex, but the old man assured him the swelling would go down after he elevated them for a while.

"Go on, Alex," he said, shedding his wet coat. "I'll be all right."

Before he left, Alex helped him onto the couch in the front room and tended the stove until it was safe to leave it. He brought the lamp into the front room and put it on the table beside the couch. The steel cash box rested on the floor within the old man's reach.

"Okay?" he asked.

The old man nodded. "Go home, Alex. It's much too late."

Alex saw the exhaustion on the old man's face and wondered what could be in the steel box so precious that the old man had risked death to fetch it back.

"Good night," Alex said.

"Good night, Alex. Thank you."

Outside the night was different now that he was alone. The wind was colder and the stars less friendly. As he hurried across the trestle and on toward home, he wondered if the demons the old man had spoken of were all dead now, or if they still wandered the tracks, ready to attach themselves to anyone foolish enough to come by.

# thirteen

The lights were on when he got home.

"Alex!" his mother cried as he came through the door. She rushed over as if to hug him, but instead, suddenly, she slapped him hard across his face. Her crying then seemed to come from deep inside her. He looked past her toward his father, who loomed large and angry beside the dining table. When he put down his cup of coffee, it broke the saucer in half.

"Where the hell have you been?" he demanded.

"We thought you were drowned or lost in the swamp," his mother said through her tears. "We called Chief Bicks . . ."

His father wheeled on his heels and disappeared into the front room. Alex could hear him on the telephone, probably talking to Chief Bicks. Alex struggled to find something to say that would make things right with his parents.

"I had to help Mr. Turner," he said at last.

"Do what?" his mother asked incredulously. His father had returned from the front room and was staring at him.

"Go get something in West Milton Falls." He told them as few of the facts as he thought he could get away with, but even then he felt as if he were violating a trust between himself and the old man. His parents did not understand—neither what he told them, nor the things he left out.

"You're grounded for a week," his father said. "You've been spending far too much time with that old man. Your mother and I have felt this all along. Now he'll just have to get by without you for a while."

Alex stood then and took every word of the lecture he had coming, until his father, at least, had said everything that was on his mind.

"Go to bed!" he finished at last.

"You must be starved," his mother said, trying to end the anger.

Alex shook his head. His stomach had ached so long with emptiness he felt sick, but he wanted to get away from them.

"Let me fix you something," his mother insisted.

"Will you stop babying him!" his father exploded.

Under cover of this diversion, Alex stole past them and up the stairs to his room.

Alex thought often about the old man during the week he was grounded. Several times he was on the verge of disobeying orders and sneaking down to the tracks after school to see how the old man was doing. Only the fear that, if he did, he would be permanently kept from visiting the hermit stopped him from going. His parents watched him closely; his mother tried to talk to him; he behaved like a model prisoner.

But he could not forget how tired the old man had looked upon their return to Fog Hollow Station—the swelling in his legs and ankles, the weariness in his face, the difficulty he had breathing. Alex wanted to shout at his parents that they were wrong to keep him away from the old man. But they couldn't understand, and if he lost control, he would jeopardize any chance he had of seeing the old man once his punishment was over.

Chief Bicks was waiting for him in his truck Tuesday afternoon after school and waved him over from the bus ramp.

"Hey, there, Alex! Come on, I'll drive you home."

Alex climbed into the truck and they pulled out of the school yard. Chief Bicks still needed a shave—it was never a beard that he wore, but three days' growth of whiskers every time Alex saw him.

"How are things going, Alex, me boy?" Chief Bicks asked. The pickup lurched toward the highway.

"Okay," Alex told him.

"A little rough at school?"

Alex wondered how much he knew. "A little."

"They're not bad kids. Just a trifle narrow-minded, like their parents. They'll warm to you in time."

Alex shrugged, as if he didn't care if they ever did.

Chief Bicks grinned at him, but the gray eyes still regarded him without humor. "Had a little ruckus with your folks the other day?"

"Yeah."

They were driving fast along the highway, through swirls of red and yellow leaves that had blown in from the sides of the road. Chief Bicks laughed.

"What the hell time did you get in, anyway?"

"When my father called you," Alex said. He wanted to end the joking. If Chief Bicks wanted to lecture him too, he could get on with it without the long buildup.

But there was no real lecture on the chief's mind. "You and the old man have become good friends, I gather."

"Yeah."

"I'm glad, Alex. I'm glad you can see him as he really is and not as some sort of freak." The chief drove past Four Corners and turned onto the dirt road north toward his house.

"But your folks worry about you, is all, Alex. They just worry."

"I know."

Chief Bicks nodded. "Long as you know that. You're lucky they care that much. You can't expect them to understand everything you're up to."

The chief laughed when he saw the look on Alex's face. "No preaching, Alex, me boy. Just words between friends, okay?"

Alex nodded. "Okay."


Alex was surprised the next day when Fritz sat down next to him on the bus ride home from school. Alex usually had a seat all to himself.

"Want to talk to you," Fritz told him, his voice low and secretive. His deep brown eyes studied Alex closely, as if looking for a weak spot.

"What do you want?" Alex asked him.

"Things could go a lot easier for you at school if you was to cut out your stuck-up ways a little and try to get along."

Alex said nothing.

"I mean, if you helped me with something, I could get some of the guys at school off your back." Fritz grinned wickedly at him. "Then with all your natural charm, I know you could make some friends."

"What do you want?" Alex repeated.

Fritz seemed a bit set back by Alex's directness. But he plunged ahead anyway. "Well, you and old man Turner are real buddies now."

"So?"

"So you must know where he keeps his collection of silver coins. All you got to do is slip us the word, tell us where to look."

Alex pushed Fritz so hard, he fell into the aisle. "Go to hell," Alex told him. "Just take your ideas and go to hell with them."

Hate blazed in Fritz's eyes, turning them to brown fire. He stood up slowly and went to the front of the bus.

Alex looked out the bus window at the fields and trees. He thought of the old man at Fog Hollow Station and of Thoreau alone at Walden Woods. He imagined himself at the edge of the pond talking with Thoreau, and he slipped so deeply into his fantasy that the bus driver had to shout at him when they came to his stop.

# fourteen

His grounding was over on Sunday, and he hurried through his work with his father, impatient to be away. When finally they were finished working on the storm windows, his father grabbed his arm to stop him.

"I suppose you're off to see the hermit?"

Alex nodded, fearful that a further punishment was to come, already choking on the injustice of it.

"You're treading a thin line, Alex," his father said. "Cross it again and you'll force my hand."

Alex didn't ask him to explain. He nodded and waited to be released. Finally his father let him go and watched him race down the yard toward the tracks. He was still gazing after him when Alex turned at the tracks to look back.

He hurried toward Fog Hollow Station. A storm the night

before had blown away many of the leaves, and some trees were nearly bare already. The woods were becoming lean, thinning toward their winter skeletons, and the wind now wasn't the balmy breeze of Indian summer but a chill foretaste of the November blasts to come.

Alex saw no smoke coming from the chimney of the station and raced on in fear. He entered through the rear door without knocking and stopped short when he saw the old man sitting at his kitchen table looking through the contents of the steel cash box. The table was cluttered with pages of letters and old, faded photographs. The old man quickly gathered them up and returned them to a canvas pouch, which he then replaced in the steel box. He locked the padlock and pocketed the key.

"It's cold in here," Alex said lamely. "Your fire's out."

"So it is," the old man said. "I lost track of myself." His voice was hoarse with a cold, and Alex noticed when he stood up to go to the stove that his feet were encased in several pairs of socks instead of shoes.

"I couldn't come sooner," Alex told him as the old man bent to his fire. "My folks made me stay in for a week."

"Because you got home so late?"

"Yeah."

"Well, Alex, I don't want to come between you and your parents."

Alex was afraid for a moment that he was going to tell him not to come anymore, but he smiled instead. "So I guess we'll take no more all-night tramps together."

He threw some dry wood on the flames, then stood back to see if it would catch. The stove began to crack and snap with heat.

"That's okay," Alex said. "I'm glad we went, though."

He glanced at the locked steel box on the table. "Was everything in it?"

The old man nodded. "Everything as I left it." He looked at Alex. "I was hoping you'd come yesterday, but today is just as good. I'd like with your help to bring in the rest of my winter apples."

"Where are they?"

"In the field behind the station. There are two apple trees remaining from somebody's orchard. I take whatever they give me each year, cut out the worms and savor the rest."

Alex carried the two empty bushel baskets and was horrified to see the old man start out without any shoes. When he called out, the old man waved his hand impatiently. "Nothing fits. The socks will do."

He led the way onto a path behind the station, but instead of heading toward the pond, he turned right, onto higher ground, and they walked for a distance through a grove of young beech trees. Suddenly the old man stopped short.

"Crouch down, Alex," he whispered. "And move very quietly."

Puzzled, Alex did as he was told. Together they crept through the hardwood forest until they came to the edge of a small clearing. Three deer stood under the apple trees feeding on windfalls. They had neither heard nor smelled their approach.

"This wind will keep them from smelling us," the old man whispered. His nose was running, but he paid no attention. "They can spot movement easily, so keep as still as you can."

Alex crouched there at the edge of the woods and watched the deer. He had never seen wild deer before, and he felt a thrill he couldn't name bursting inside him, a kind of joy.

"The one nearest us is the doe," the old man told him. "The large one behind her with the small set of antlers is a yearling, probably her buck fawn from last year. The smallest one is this year's fawn."

Alex watched them intently. From time to time the doe would raise her head and look about and sniff the wind, and then the others would follow her example. They ate the apples with obvious relish, and the old man smiled and nodded slightly toward them.

"They know winter's coming," he said softly. "They've got to fatten up for the winter yard. Even the fawn knows that, and it has never seen a winter yet."

Suddenly the doe raised her head again, more alertly than before. With a sudden bound she took to the cover of the trees beyond the tiny orchard. The others followed. In a moment they were gone.

"What frightened them?" Alex asked, still filled with the wonder of their flight to safety. He stood up slowly. "Did they see us?"

The old man shook his head and took out a handkerchief. He wiped at his nose and at his eyes, which were swollen with tears from his cold. "Hard to say, Alex. Something else in the woods might have startled them, something we didn't even hear. Except for their sight, they have far better senses than we have."

He looked toward the apple trees. "Let's go see what they've left for me."


Alex climbed up and pulled down what he could reach of the apples that were left on the branches. He didn't think that they looked like much—small and wrinkled and full of blemishes that probably spoke of the worms inside—but the old man was eager for all they could gather.

"I'll make sauce of the ones I can't eat," he said. "It's foolish to be so proud you turn up your nose at what nature offers you."

They nearly filled one of the bushel baskets. "We'll leave the windfalls for the deer," the old man said. Together they walked slowly back toward the station, Alex carrying the apples. He noticed that the old man was limping, but he said nothing.

When the station was in sight, the old man stopped. "That's strange, Alex. I know I didn't leave that door open."

Alex saw the back door gaping open and hurried to follow the old man the rest of the way down to the station. He reached the back steps first and pounded up them and inside the kitchen. He saw no one inside and looked around quickly for any sign someone had been there. But it was the old man, when he finally puffed his way into the kitchen all out of breath, who saw immediately what had been taken.

"The box!" he cried. "They've stolen my box!"

Alex looked at the table. The old man's steel cash box was gone.

# fifteen

The old man stood there as if a blow to his stomach had knocked out his wind. Alex took one look at his face, at his eyes like pools of sadness, and knew that he had to act. He had a good idea who had stolen the box and where they had taken it. He would bring it back to the old man.

"I'll get it!" he told him. "I promise I will. I know who stole it."

Without looking back, he left the station and ran to the tracks. He pounded over the ties toward Fritz's and Benny's secret swimming hole. The stream ran high beside him, full of the fall rains, but he paid no attention to it. Up ahead he could see the grove of tall trees that hid the pool, and he ran even faster to the path that cut into the grove, and only once he was on that path did he think of stealth and slow down his headlong rush.

He bent over to catch his breath and rest his aching sides. He heard nothing but his own hard breathing and, beyond it, the rush of the stream as it raced its way to the pool. Slowly, carefully, he stepped forward. He had to catch them by surprise.

The wind rattled the trees above him, and a steady cascade of brown and scarlet leaves fell over him. The stream was swollen, the pool high. Alex saw that Fritz and Benny had added more boards to their hut on the other side of the swimming hole. He saw movement through the gaps in the wall and knew they were inside.

In summer the way across the stream was a pathway of boulders just upstream from the pool, but now, in this time of high water, these boulders were under water. He had to wade across, his feet turning to ice through his sneakers. He slipped once, nearly lost his balance, and was soaked to his thighs by the time he reached the other side.

He shook away the cold and made his way toward the hut. The wind overhead covered the noise his steps made on the leaf-strewn ground. He heard pounding from the hut, and soon he was close enough to see between the boards. Both boys were bent over the steel cash box, and Fritz was beating the latch with a rock.

While Alex watched, the lock suddenly gave and the lid of the box flipped up as the box tipped over on its side. In a moment Fritz had yanked up the canvas pouch and dumped its contents on the ground. His swearing then was loud and furious.

"Junk!" he screamed. "It's nothing but goddamn junk!"

He leafed violently through the letters and photographs. He picked up the cash box and peered into its emptiness as if it might still hold the promised treasure. Then he flung it against one wall of the hut, just inches from Alex's face.

"Where's the silver?" Benny asked.

"Where's the silver?" Fritz screamed back at him. "It's not here, stupid, that's for sure. I told you we should have looked around more while we were in there. But no, you had to get chicken."

"Well, they might have come back," Benny argued.

"Now what have we got?" Fritz demanded. "Nothing, nothing but dumb old letters." He picked up a packet of envelopes as if he meant to take out his rage on them by shredding them into little pieces. Alex had no time to think— he had to save the old man's memories.

He pushed hard on the side of the hut, grabbed at one of the boards that braced up the wall, and pushed again. Boards creaked loudly as the side of the hut sagged inward. Alex yelled as rage escaped inside him and bubbled to the surface. One more push brought the whole hut down, and he picked up the now unattached brace and rushed around to the front of the hut, shouting in triumph.

He began banging on the pile of lumber that had once been Fritz's and Benny's hideaway. As the two of them scrambled out from under the wreckage, he saw the look of shock and terror on their faces. Shouting continuously at the top of his voice, he kept beating on the boards until he realized that the plank in his hands was now no more than a stump of wood.

Looking around, he saw that Fritz and Benny had run off without a fight, totally terrorized. As reason began to trickle back into his mind, he understood that he had to act quickly before they had time to regain their courage. Pushing away the boards, he dug through the ruins of the hut until he found the cash box. Carefully he replaced all the packets of letters and the photographs, trying hard not to look at any of them. There wasn't time, and besides, a strong sense of the old man's need and right to privacy possessed him. If he looked through these private papers, these precious bits of the old man's past, then he'd be little better than Fritz and Benny.

But one photograph caught his eye; a picture of a young woman so beautiful that even through the sense of time gone by, despite the old-fashioned clothes and the yellowed photograph itself, she still seemed to speak to him, to take his breath away. Quickly he placed her picture with the others and put them in the canvas pouch.

When he had retrieved everything, he tucked the box securely under his arm and stood up. He saw nothing in the woods as he looked around, but he sensed that Fritz and Benny hadn't gone far. He hurried to the head of the pool and waded back across the stream.

Behind him the hut lay in ruins. His enemies no doubt watched him go, storing up their hatred for another day. But he had won the battle, and the old man's box was safe again.

The old man was sitting at his table, his face in his hands. The station was so silent the ticking of the clock ruled over everything. Gently, Alex placed the battered cash box beside him on the table.

"It's all here, Mr. Turner," Alex told him. "The box is kind of demolished. But I got back everything."

Slowly the old man opened the box and looked into the canvas bag, but he did not remove the contents.

"It's really all there," Alex repeated. "I'm sure of it."

The old man nodded absently. It was as if he were half asleep.

"Well, you'll probably want to check it over after I leave." Alex said uncertainly. He backed slowly away from the table. "I've got to go now, Mr. Turner. It's getting late."

The old man nodded again. "Thank you, Alex," he said. But he was looking toward the blank wall, as if it were a window onto something only he could see.

"I'll come by again soon," Alex called and hurried from the station. On the way home he cried and he wasn't sure why.

# sixteen

The old man was not the same after his box was stolen and broken into. Like a violation of his most private self, it seemed to leave him burned out and empty.

Alex came to see him as often as he could, as often as his schoolwork and his parents and the renovation work on the farmhouse would allow him to. He would rebuild the fire in the stove and bring in fresh piles of firewood and light the kerosene lamp when evening came, just before he left for home.

On some afternoons he read to the old man from Thoreau's *Walden*, but it became less and less clear whether the old man heard the words or paid much attention to them. His cold grew worse and settled in his chest; the swelling in his legs never went down.

"I'll call your sister," Alex told him one day. "Maybe you should go into the hospital for a while."

The old man turned to him when he heard these words and shook his head. His eyes cleared as he made the effort to understand and to be understood.

"No, Alex. Promise me you'll call no one. I want to stay here.".

And locked again in the look of those eyes, Alex had to promise what the old man wanted.

For the next few days the old man fought to hold onto this clarity. They talked again of the passages Alex read aloud in *Walden*, and the old man again studied the letters and photographs in the steel box.

October passed into November and the edge of winter grew closer. One Saturday morning when ice had formed on the borders of the stream and the water passing under the trestle rang with a different, bell-like note, Alex walked to the station, his breath like a cloud before him, and found the old man lying still on the couch in the front room. He talked to him for several moments before he realized that the old man was dead, and then he just stood there as still as ice himself.

At last he roused himself from his numbness and forced himself to go to the old man and check for a pulse. There was none, no breathing, no life at all, just a note that Alex had to tug free.

"Take the box, Alex," he read.

Alex carried the steel cash box home and hid it in his closet and then called Chief Bicks himself and went back to the station to wait for him to get there. He waited outside until the chief got there. He stayed until the old man had been taken away.

During the days that followed Alex thought a lot about the old man. The steel box sat unopened in his closet. Maybe someday he would open it and read its contents and put together the missing pieces of the old man's life, but not now. Not now while his own memories were so close and fresh.

When he thought of the old man, he remembered High Meadow and the first trout he had ever caught. He remembered *Walden* and Thoreau, and how he and the old man had argued through the rainy days of September. The more fierce the argument, the more the old man had delighted in it.

He remembered the long walk to retrieve the steel cash box in West Milton Falls and how, on the long walk back, the old man had pointed out Polaris, the North Star, and told him it always maintained its place in the night sky. He remembered the few glimpses he had had of the old man's earlier life, and he remembered the deer eating apples in the orchard behind Fog Hollow Station, preparing for their winter yard.

And every night when the freight train roared by, blowing for each crossing, Alex thought of the old man and remembered all the wonderful things the old man had given him, and wished him well, wished him peace.